When Cats Dream

Story and Paintings by

DAV PILKEY

Orchard Books   New York

Orchard Books, 95 Madison Avenue, New York, NY 10016

Manufactured in the United States of America. Printed by Barton Press, Inc.
Bound by Horowitz/Rae. Book design by Mina Greenstein.
The text of this book is set in 18 point Usherwood Medium.
The illustrations are watercolor with pencil, reproduced in full color.   10 9 8 7 6 5 4 3 2 1

Library of Congress Cataloging-in-Publication Data   E PIL
Pilkey, Dav, date. When cats dream / story and paintings by Dav Pilkey.   p.   cm.
"A Richard Jackson book." Summary: When cats dream, they can do anything they want, from
combing their hair with the moon to swinging from vines in the jungle.
ISBN 0-531-05997-9.   ISBN 0-531-08597-X (lib. bdg.)
[1. Cats—Fiction. 2. Dreams—Fiction.] I. Title. PZ7.P63123Wh 1992
[E]—dc20   91-31355

OCLC: 24320332

For TOMATO,
who came to us
in our dreams

When cats are awake,
all the world is the same.

The food is always in the same corner. . . .

The ball is always under
the wooden chair. . . .

And there are always big people
with softwarm laps
to be in.

But when cats go to sleep,
everything begins to change.
The white walls become blue,
and the curtains blow inside out.

The world is getting deeper.
And all the noises are small.

Nothing is the same when cats dream.
The moonbeams come in the window,
swish, swish. . . .

The fishbowl is now an ocean,
and cats can dive in.

When cats are dreaming,
they can swim with the fishes
and lose their socks in the sea.

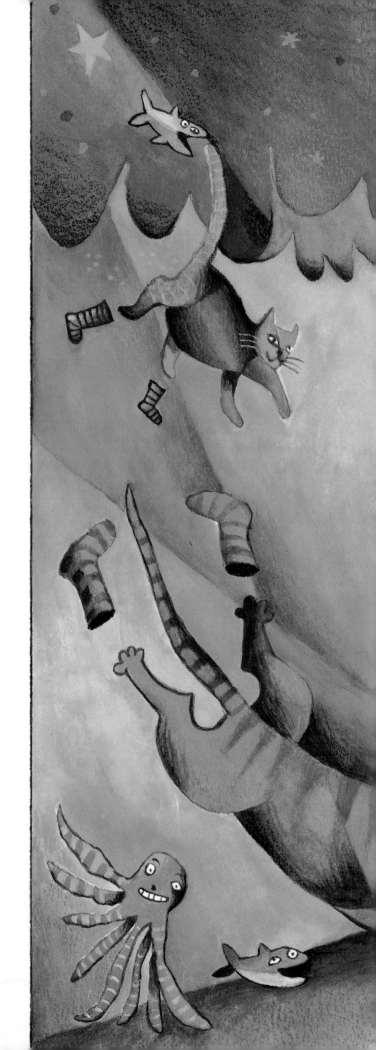

When cats dream,
someone always has
left the back door open,
and no cat is afraid.

The big orange dog that lives outside is asleep,
snoring, snoring, snoring.
And cats can dance on his head.

The world is not so big now.
Cats fly in the air.
If they want to, they can wear shoes.
And a tie.

They can eat up the sun
and swallow the stars.
When cats are dreaming,
they can comb their hair with the moon.

And later, when the clouds are soft and marbled,

those dreaming cats will find their way to the jungle.

Out in the deep jungle
there are lots of cats,
stalking.
And swinging from vines.
Still they are asleep,
and there is dreaming going on.

And while they are there,
some grass reaches up
to tickle the pads of their feet,

and cats must go home.
Running, running, running.

When you are a cat who dreams,
the whole world smells like you.
The other cats sing songs about you.

You can lie in the pasture with quilts.
You can be the only one in the world.

Until the smell of rain comes
in the curtains,
and cats must wake up.

And when cats are awake,
when they stop their dreaming
and everything once again is the same,
they can eat some food
from the dish in the corner. . . .

They can look at the ball
under the wooden chair. . . .

And after a time,
they can find another softwarm lap
to be in. . . .

And cats can go back to their dreaming.